STADIUM SCHOOL

WHERE FOOTBALLING DREAMS COME TRUE

Hot
Prospect

Jefferies & Goffe

A & C Black • London

To Cindy, who I quite literally couldn't have done it without, and to Cat, for living with my football madness. SG

Thanks to Seb, who has made our writing partnership so much fun. CJ

First published 2008 by
A & C Black Publishers Ltd
38 Soho Square, London, W1D 3HB

www.acblack.com

Text copyright © 2008 C. Jefferies and S. Goffe

ISBN 978-0-7136-8885-6

A CIP catalogue for this book is available from the British Library.

This book is produced using paper that is made from wood grown in managed, sustainable forests. It is natural, renewable and recyclable. The logging and manufacturing processes conform to the environmental regulations of the country of origin.

Printed and bound in Great Britain by CPI Cox & Wyman, Reading, RG1 8EX

Hot
Prospect

Contents

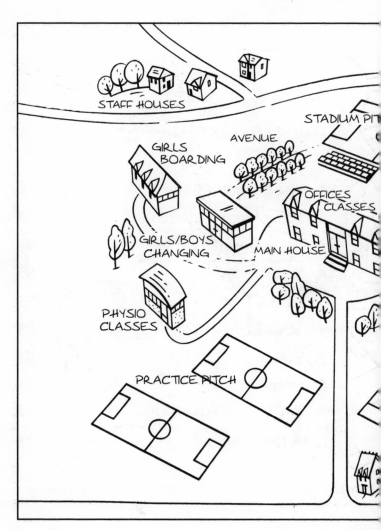

STAFF HOUSES

STADIUM PIT

AVENUE

GIRLS
BOARDING

OFFICES
CLASSES

GIRLS/BOYS
CHANGING

MAIN HOUSE

PHYSIO
CLASSES

PRACTICE PITCH

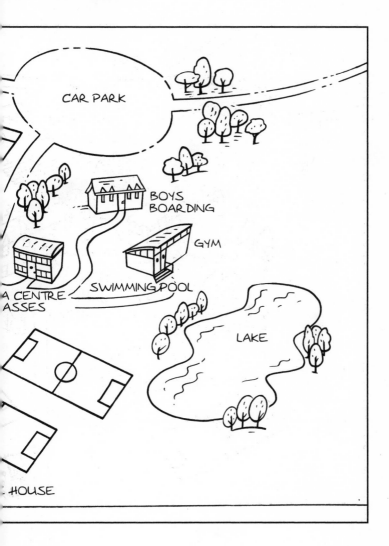

CAR PARK

BOYS BOARDING

GYM

A CENTRE
ASSES

SWIMMING POOL

LAKE

HOUSE

1. The Beautiful Game

"Roddy! Your ball!"

Roddy Jones turned and chased the goalie's wayward kick up the pitch. He was exhausted from running himself into the ground all afternoon for the Valley Primary School team, but happy doing what he absolutely loved. He was easily the best player, and as captain did most of the work himself, but he didn't care. In his head he was a world-famous attacking midfielder, playing in the World Cup, and he could hear the commentators marvelling at his skill.

And it's Jones now, in acres of space. He puts his foot on the ball and looks up to assess the situation, then spots Bryn Thomas making

Hot Prospect

a lovely run down the right wing. He hoists a pin-point pass 40 yards across the pitch, and sets off at a gallop towards the penalty area. Thomas collects the ball a split second before the covering defender, and instinctively lashes in a cross to where he knows Jones will be arriving. Without breaking his stride, the young Welsh-Brazilian midfielder lets the ball bounce once before firing home a vicious half-volley into the top-left corner, leaving the despairing keeper sprawled in the mud. Jones wheels away with his fist in the air, and slides on his knees towards the corner flag. His fourth goal seals a magnificent 5–1 victory for a well-deserved place in the final!

Roddy came off the field with the rest of his five-a-side team. He was gasping for breath, covered in mud, and his jet-black hair was sticky with sweat. But his dark eyes were sparkling with excitement, and he was laughing. They'd won every game they'd played and were in the final of the tournament. What could possibly be better than that?

"Stuffed them, didn't we, Bryn?" Roddy panted to his best mate with glee, rubbing his face with the bottom of his shirt.

Bryn Thomas nodded his cropped head. "St David's has twice as many pupils as we do," he said. "But they're useless."

"Now then," said their coach, Mr Taylor, as he joined them from the touchline. "No rubbishing the opposition."

"But 5–1!" objected Bryn. "They *are* useless."

"They just don't have a Roddy Jones," said Mr Taylor, smiling at the team. "He played a blinder out there, but he needs more support. This is a team game. You can't expect Roddy to do all the work. You're in the final now, but if you're not careful, our star player won't survive the match."

"Drinks! And a Mars bar each." It was Roddy's dad with the refreshments. Dan Jones was almost as keen on football as his son, and had taken the afternoon off to help with the five-a-side tournament. "Well done, Roddy," he added proudly. "Your third goal was brilliant. I think St David's gave up after that. Well done, all of you."

"Yes, you've earned your place in the final," agreed Mr Taylor. "And we're playing on this pitch again, so you can have a good rest. The opposition will have to come to us."

"Who are we up against?" asked Roddy between gulps of his drink. He was sorry the day was almost over, despite being totally shattered. His mum, Francesca Jones, said he was so football mad he'd play in his sleep

The Beautiful Game

if he could! In fact, the whole family was keen on the game, but recently his older sister Liz had lost interest, which was a shame because she'd been pretty good, too.

Roddy played football whenever and wherever he got the chance. In school, in the back garden, at the park, even in his bedroom sometimes, although that wasn't really to be recommended. Roddy Jones simply *lived* for the game. Mr Taylor had already told him how much he'd be missed when he moved up to Valley Comp next term.

"You're facing Manor Primary," said Mr Taylor, checking his list. "They've only dropped one game today. Did you get a chance to see how they play, Dan?"

Roddy's dad nodded. "They've got a midfielder you'll need to watch out for," he told the team. "He's almost as quick as you, Roddy. But their defence is a bit weak – they all

Hot Prospect

want to be goal scorers. If you can get past that midfielder, you should be OK."

"Bryn, make sure you back up Roddy, and Ella, more of those long passes would be excellent," said their coach. "Manor Primary must be good, otherwise they wouldn't be in the final, but we can beat them if we play our best." He rubbed his hands together. "Time to go. Good luck, everyone."

All the parents, teachers and pupils from the losing teams were making their way over to watch. Roddy pulled his socks well up and checked the laces on his boots. He took a few deep breaths. The Manor Primary team had arrived, and the referee was ready.

Valley Primary, in red, lined up opposite the Manor Primary players in blue, both sizing each other up. With only ten minutes of football between him and the chance to lift a real trophy, Roddy wasn't going to let any of his team-mates slack off now.

"You heard Mr Taylor," he said. "The way to beat this lot is to let them come at us, then strike when they're exposed at the back. Strong defence and counterattacking, that's the stuff. Now, let's show them how to play!"

From the kickoff, Manor Primary have made their intentions clear, and are really going at the red defence, forcing Jones back to help out his team-mates. But with such a fierce assault, Manor is leaving dangerous gaps at the back, and Jones will look to take full advantage.

The reds' goalie manages to hold onto the muddy ball, and launches it over the heads of the Manor team, to where Jones is sprinting into unmarked space. The blues are streaming back to chase him, and gaining on the lone attacker. Jones has run his heart out today, and with the rain beginning to come down,

Hot Prospect

his pace is fading. Just as he shapes to shoot, a blue shirt catches up and clatters into him from behind, clearly with no intention of playing the ball. The ref's whistle shrills immediately, and he gives the defender a good talking to, but the free kick comes to nothing and the chance is wasted.

The reds are back struggling in their own half, unable to play under the constant pressure from the blues. As the first half draws to a close, the reds seem to be cracking. The ball is floated in from the flanks, and Flowers, in the Valley goal, only succeeds in punching as far as the blue midfielder lurking on the edge of the box, who avoids a tackle, and slots the ball into the bottom corner of the net. 1–0 to Manor Primary. The ref looks at his watch, and blows a long blast to signal the end of the half.

There was a short rest before play began again.

The Beautiful Game

"You all right, mate?" Bryn asked Roddy anxiously. "That was a horrible tackle. He should've been sent off."

"I'm fine," said Roddy. "It's just a pity we didn't get a goal out of it."

Ella Flowers was sitting on her own, blaming herself for the ball she'd let in, but Roddy did his bit to cheer her up.

"Come on," he said. "One goal will get us back in the game, and they'll be rattled then. We can still win this!"

The ref was waving them back onto the pitch, and Roddy's monologue resumed.

The reds have left themselves a mountain to climb, but if anyone can inspire a reversal of fortunes, it's Jones. He plays the ball out to Thomas, in his customary position wide on the right, and moves up the pitch in unison with his vice-captain.

Thomas splits the defence with a magical

Hot Prospect

through-ball, leaving Jones one on one with the keeper. He runs forward until he can see the whites of the goalie's eyes. Then, with a cheeky little shimmy, he leaves the keeper sprawling as the ball spins into the back of the net. Jones wheels away to high-five his team-mates, then jogs back to his own half to await the restart. 1–1. Can either side finish this?

The clock was winding down, and the match looked like heading to penalties. Neither side was dominating, and all ten players were exhausted. Roddy picked up the ball on the edge of his own area after another fruitless blue attack, and saw an open space ahead of him.

And now Jones is on the ball. It's a long way to the other end, but he's thundering down the pitch. He skips past the despairing lunge of the only blue defender, and now he is all alone in the Manor Primary half.

The Beautiful Game

Jones puts his head down and hoofs the ball ahead of himself, sprinting to catch up. The keeper is unsure what to do, and dithers a few yards off his line before rushing out late. Jones senses the indecision, and hoists a perfect lob. Time seems to stand still as the ball arcs over the goalie's outstretched hands. Slowly, it dips just under the crossbar and nestles in the back of the net. The final whistle goes! Jones topples over backwards and lies flat out on the ground, before being crushed by his celebrating team-mates. Manor Primary is gutted. Jones will be lifting the cup here, and his team will be taking home the glory!

Valley Primary was presented with prizes by the tournament sponsor. There was a silver cup for their school and a boot bag for each member of the team. Roddy raised the cup above his head to the cheers of the crowd. As the applause died away, he could see his dad smiling proudly, so Roddy sprinted over to him. But before he could show off his winnings, Mr Taylor had joined them, too.

"I wonder if Roddy might be interested in this," he said, offering a leaflet to Roddy's dad. "There are limited places, and it's first come, first served, but I'm sure it would be worthwhile. They're a very prestigious organisation, and they haven't come to this area before."

"What is it?" asked Roddy.

Roddy's dad passed him the leaflet. "It's a one-day football summer school," he said. "Would you like to go?"

"It's run by Stadium School!" said Roddy, staring at the front of the smart, glossy flyer. "I saw a programme about them on TV."

"This isn't actually going to be held at Stadium School," Mr Taylor explained. "The summer-school day will be held at the County

The Beautiful Game

Ground in our town, but the coaches are from Stadium School. I should think you'd pick up some good tips if you went along."

Roddy looked at the leaflet again. On the front was a picture of a young player, not much older than himself, in the blue-and-green strip of the famous school. The TV programme had shown how students there had the best coaches and the most amazing facilities to help them develop a successful career in football. Leavers got picked up by clubs like Manchester United and Chelsea, and the presenter had interviewed one ex-student, who had recently been chosen to play for his country! It was the best place to be if you wanted to make it as a professional footballer, so it would be brilliant to get a taste of their coaching, even if it was just for a day. Mr Taylor and Dad were OK, but they weren't experts by any means.

Hot Prospect

"Ring the number now!" Roddy urged his dad. "Hurry, before all the places go. Please!"

Mr Jones laughed. "I'll do it as soon as we get back to the car," he said. "Thanks," he added to Mr Taylor. "It's good to find something exciting for Roddy to do in the holidays."

"Will you *really* ring straight away?" demanded Roddy impatiently.

Dan looked at Mr Taylor. "Now look what you've done," he joked. "I'm not going to get any peace until I've made that call."

"See you at the car in a minute," Roddy said. "I'm just going to tell Bryn about it. He's sure to want to go, too."

Roddy headed towards his friend, who was sitting on the ground taking off his boots. In Roddy's mind they were both at the summer school already, learning all the skills they'd need to get into the first team at Valley Comp.

The Beautiful Game

It'll be interesting to see what Jones and Thomas make of this chance. Thomas's performance can be a bit inconsistent, and Jones could do with better service from his team-mate. This is a big opportunity for them both to fine tune their skills, and make them even more of a force to be reckoned with.

Roddy wondered if anyone famous would be there. It would be so cool if a professional footballer from the Premier League came along. Sometimes they did help out at things like this. Roddy felt excited just thinking about it. Picking up some real, *expert* advice would be a dream come true. Now he just had to hope there were some places left.

2. Some Proper Coaching

Fortunately there *were* places at the summer school for both Roddy and Bryn, so the week after school finished, they caught the bus down to the County Ground. Roddy wore the Wales strip he'd been given for his last birthday, and they both carried their boots in the bags they'd won.

There were kids of all ages there. Some adult helpers sorted them out into age groups and sent them off to different parts of the field, each with a Stadium School representative. Roddy didn't notice anyone famous, but Bryn recognised someone they'd seen at the tournament.

"There's that kid from the Manor Primary

Some Proper Coaching

team!" he whispered, as they followed their representative to an empty part of the field.

Sure enough, the boy who had fouled Roddy was in their group.

Roddy shrugged. "Never mind," he said. "I expect he'll be all right. We're not in a final now."

"Hello, everyone," said the young group leader, who was wearing the stylish blue-and-green Stadium School strip that Roddy had seen on TV. "I'm Peter Denver, and I've just finished my final year at Stadium School."

Roddy couldn't hide his disappointment. "He's just a student," he muttered to Bryn. "I thought we were supposed to have a *real* coach!"

He'd meant the comment to come out quietly, but Peter obviously heard him. "Don't worry," he said, grinning in Roddy's direction. "You'll be getting plenty of input later from our juniors' coach, but I'm going to do some fun stuff with you while he's working with another group. And I can answer any questions you have about Stadium School. After all, I did go there for five years!"

"What's it like?" called out a curly-haired girl.

Peter smiled. "Brilliant!" he said. "It's so good to be at a school where everyone is crazy about the game. They even try to bring football into maths and other ordinary lessons. And being a boarding school, there's always someone to have a kick about with. I'm almost sorry to be leaving."

"Where are you going now?" asked Roddy.

"I've been signed by Blackburn Rovers," Peter told them, looking very proud. "I'll be starting in their youth squad in September."

Peter had done what Roddy could only dream about. To live and breathe football,

Some Proper Coaching

and come out of school signed to a good club. Roddy wasn't sure how he felt. Part of him was fiercely jealous, but he also felt rather in awe. More than anything, he felt challenged to do his very best today, to show Peter that even kids from *ordinary* schools could play great football.

"Come on then, let's get started," said Peter. "All in a circle for keepy-uppy. Whoever lets the ball drop is out of the game, unless they're given a bad pass. My decision is final." He dropped the ball he was carrying on to his foot and bounced it while he talked, then passed it neatly to Roddy. "Go!"

Roddy was taken by surprise. He wasn't expecting it to come to him first, but the pass was perfect and he easily had the ball under control. He flicked it across the circle to the curly-haired girl who had asked Peter a question, and was glad that his pass was given

Hot Prospect

the OK. Slowly, players began to drop out, either from trying to be too clever, or just from making mistakes. When there were only half a dozen left in the circle, Peter called an end to the game.

"All right," he said. "Excellent stuff, but that's enough. We could be here all day if we waited for some of you to mess up! Now, let's try something else."

When the juniors' coach, Mr Jenkins, came over, Peter spent a few minutes speaking to him quietly. The coach cast his gaze over the group and Roddy shivered with anticipation. The last hour had been great fun, but now they were going to be taught by someone really important. Roddy had devoured every word of the leaflet, so he knew that Mr Jenkins had played for Wales before he'd turned to coaching. That was partly why he'd decided to wear his Wales strip to the day.

Some Proper Coaching

The coach's eyes rested on Roddy for a moment and Roddy looked boldly back. He wanted the coach to see how determined he was. He might only be young, but football was his life, just as it was for any Premier League player.

"So, who here wants to be a professional footballer?" Mr Jenkins asked by way of introduction. Naturally, a chorus of "me" erupted from the group, and a smile broke across the coach's face. "And do you have what it takes? Peter here tells me you're pretty good, but it takes more than talent to make it as a pro. What else do you need?"

"Hard work!"

"Determination!"

"Luck!"

"Belief!"

"Passion!"

"All good answers," said Mr Jenkins,

Hot Prospect

holding up his hand for silence. "Especially luck. There are literally thousands of kids like you who are football crazy, thousands who have the ability. A lot of kids never get the opportunity to make the next step, and most will only have the one shot at it. It's all about grabbing the chance when you get it, making the most of every bit of luck. But today's just a bit of fun. Let's split you up into teams for a few games. How many keepers have we got?" He counted the raised hands. "Five. Excellent. Goalies go over there, defenders here, midfielders in the middle and strikers, you come over by me. Now we can make some balanced teams."

Once the players had sorted themselves out, Mr Jenkins chose teams of seven. Roddy and Bryn were split up, but Roddy didn't mind. It would be interesting to play with some different people for a change. The teams were

Some Proper Coaching

playing first to two goals and winner stays on. Roddy's team were on first. As his side put on blue bibs, Roddy spotted the Manor Primary player in the opposition. He hoped that there would be no hard feelings between them.

Rather than refereeing the game as Roddy had expected, Mr Jenkins stood on the side, sometimes calling out advice, as if he was the manager of both teams. The rest of the time he simply watched and made the occasional note, or chatted with the teams waiting to go on, leaving Peter to ref the games. Mr Jenkins had chosen the teams well, and the blues were evenly matched with their opponents.

Jones is playing with some unfamiliar faces today, but he will still be looking to shine. With his first touch of the ball he shows off his remarkable talent, whizzing past two defenders before passing to a team-mate. He receives the ball back almost instantly,

Hot Prospect

and hits a belter of a shot to score the first goal. 1–0 to the blues!

The Manor Primary pupil gave him a menacing look, and Roddy hoped he wouldn't do anything stupid.

Jones's team win the ball back straight from the kickoff, and Jones himself is just getting it under control when an opponent comes steaming in on him. That's a bad foul! The referee goes straight to his pocket and brandishes a red card. One team will be a man down for the rest of this game. Not what you want to see in a friendly match.

"Are you all right?" Peter asked, as he gave Roddy a hand up.

"I'll live," replied Roddy. "That kid's an idiot. My school beat his in the final of a tournament last week."

"Well, there's no place for grudges on the pitch. Mr Jenkins will soon sort him out."

Some Proper Coaching

There's a severe earbashing being handed out by the coach. The referee blows to restart the game. Harpendon takes the free kick, and the wayward pass has left a loose ball. Jones puts his head down and tries to make amends. He's going like a steam train to get to it first! His level of commitment is fantas— Now that's a real pity. I don't think there was any malice in it, but it's a clear foul.

Roddy felt an impact on his elbow and turned around to see a slightly built, brown-haired girl lying on the ground clutching her face. Peter blew his whistle to stop the game, and gave the other team a free kick.

"Don't *you* start fouling now," he told Roddy. "She could have been badly hurt."

"I'm sorry," said Roddy, "I didn't mean—"

"I'm sure you didn't," said Peter. "But be more careful!"

For the rest of the game, Roddy kept

Hot Prospect

himself in check, but he still tried to play with as much passion as he could. His team won three games in a row before they were eventually beaten, and then Bryn's team went on.

"Well done, mate," said Bryn as Roddy handed over his bib. "You're playing brilliantly."

"Thanks," replied Roddy. "Good luck."

The time flew past. When they eventually stopped for a break, Roddy and Bryn were starving, and very hot. Everyone lay around in the shade, chatting, and ate their packed lunches. Then, after they'd eaten, they played another couple of matches. Mr Jenkins was great at giving out advice, and Roddy could have listened to him for ever, but all too soon he and Bryn were back in the changing rooms.

"That was great, wasn't it?" said Bryn, as they packed away their boots. "I wish it could

Some Proper Coaching

have been for more than one day though."

"It was brilliant," Roddy agreed, popping the lid of his last can of drink and swallowing a large mouthful. "I'm going to work really hard on ball control through the holiday. Do you fancy coming round tomorrow?"

"You're on," agreed Bryn. "I thought I might ask for some practice cones for my birthday. They would be better than dribbling balls round our school bags and jumpers."

"Good idea," said Roddy. He crumpled the empty can, and added it to the already overflowing rubbish bin. "Shall we go and have another quick chat with Peter? It'll be our last chance. Dad's going to be here soon."

"OK," agreed Bryn, stuffing his sweaty football socks in his bag.

They headed out of the changing rooms and saw Peter coming their way.

"All right, lads?" he said as they met.

Hot Prospect

Roddy and Bryn nodded. It was so good to be on speaking terms with a Blackburn Rovers player!

"Actually, I was looking for you," Peter told Roddy. "Mr Jenkins wants a word."

Roddy and Bryn looked at each other. In their experience, teachers only wanted to see you when you were in trouble. Roddy wondered if it was about the girl he'd knocked over. He hadn't meant to barge into her, but maybe Mr Jenkins hadn't seen it that way. He'd certainly given the Manor Primary boy a good talking-to. The last thing Roddy wanted was a telling off to sour his enjoyable day, but it looked as if he was about to get one.

Bryn slapped him sympathetically on the back. "See you in a minute," he said.

Roddy followed Peter back into the building. The older boy tapped on the nearest door and pushed it open. Mr Jenkins was in

Some Proper Coaching

there, talking to the helpers.

Roddy wondered if it would be better to try to defend himself, or simply accept the telling off. He hated to think that the coach might consider him to be a troublemaker.

"Ah! The boy with the Wales strip," said Mr Jenkins, as Roddy entered the room. "Roddy Jones, isn't it?"

"Yes," said Roddy. It was horrible when teachers started off cheerfully, as if they weren't really annoyed.

"You want to play for Wales one day, is that right?"

"Yeah," Roddy said cautiously, wondering where it was leading. "That would be a dream come true."

"Well, I wanted to let you know that we were really impressed with you today," said Mr Jenkins. "You've definitely got something."

Hot Prospect

Roddy looked at the coach in surprise. "I thought you were going to tell me off," he said before he could stop himself.

"Did you?" Mr Jenkins looked confused for a moment, and then his expression cleared. "Oh! You mean the girl you knocked over? Don't worry, these things happen. It's all a matter of awareness, and you were so focused on getting the ball, I imagine you weren't thinking of much else."

Roddy nodded thankfully. "That's it," he agreed. "I try to notice where all the players are, but sometimes I forget."

"Well, it's something you can work on," said the coach. "But that isn't why I wanted to speak to you. You see, we'd like to give you a proper trial, if you and your parents agree."

"Really?" Roddy was puzzled. "What do you mean?"

"We think you've got a lot of talent,

Some Proper Coaching

Roddy," said Mr Jenkins. "The sort of talent that would be a real asset at Stadium School. I can't say you'd be a dead cert for a place, but we're trying out some promising kids in a couple of weeks' time. If you'd like to join the group, I think you'd have a good chance of getting into the school."

Roddy's mouth fell open. "Me? At Stadium School? Like Peter?"

"That's right," said Mr Jenkins. "If you're good enough on the day. Would you like that?"

Roddy could only nod. His heart had started pounding in his chest. It was such a big thing to take in.

Mr Jenkins clapped him on the shoulder. "All right, lad," he said kindly. "Is your dad coming to collect you? I'd like to have a word. I'll come out in a minute. Don't go until I've had a chance to speak to him."

Hot Prospect

Roddy went back outside to where Bryn was waiting.

"How did it go?" asked Bryn.

"He wants me to go for a trial," explained Roddy in a daze, still finding it hard to believe. "It looks like I've got a chance of getting into Stadium School!"

Bryn laughed. "Yeah right," he said. "Pull the other one."

"No, really!" said Roddy. "They want to speak to my dad and everything. It's not a wind up, honest!"

"Honest?"

"Honest! Look, there's Dad now. I'd better go and tell him."

Roddy could feel his friend's eyes following him as he went to meet his dad. He didn't blame Bryn for not believing him. It was incredible. If he went to this trial, and if he got through, *he* could be wearing that cool

Some Proper Coaching

blue-and-green strip in the autumn, instead of starting at Valley Comp. This was one of those rare opportunities Mr Jenkins had talked about. And it had come to *him*!

In spite of the hot weather, Roddy felt a shiver run up his spine. There was no way he would let this chance pass him by. No, Roddy Jones was going to do everything he could to earn a place at Stadium School.

3. A Big Decision

At home, they spent the whole evening discussing what had happened. His parents wanted to know exactly how Roddy had been singled out as possible Stadium School material.

"I don't *know* how," said Roddy for the umpteenth time. "I was just playing football like I always do."

"Well, they must have seen your potential," said his dad. "To be picked out like that is amazing! And that coach fellow said you were the only one. I'm really proud of you, Roddy."

"So am I, love," said his mum, giving Roddy a hug. "Perhaps being half Brazilian helps," she teased. "But this is a big step, Roddy.

A Big Decision

If you got into this school, football wouldn't just be a bit of fun any more. You'd be expected to take it seriously."

"She's right, son," said his dad. "You'd have to train every day, and work at your game like a job. It's a big decision. Do you *really* want football to dominate your life?"

Roddy stared at his parents. "Of course I do!" he burst out. "It's *always* been more than a bit of fun for me. Can't you see that?"

Mr Jones smiled. "I can see it means everything to you right now," he said.

"And it always will," said Roddy seriously. "It's all I've ever wanted to do."

"Well, OK," agreed his dad. "I can see you need to go for the trial, and we're with you all the way, but we don't want you to be too disappointed if you don't succeed. You must be realistic about your chances."

"And if you did get in, you wouldn't

Hot Prospect

be able to come home whenever you felt like it," said his mum. "Stadium School is *miles* away."

Roddy tried hard to think about what it would be like to live at a school and only see his family during the holidays, but all he could think about was the trial. What would they make him do? How could he best practise for it? Did he *really* have a decent chance of getting in?

"Well?" said his mum. "What do you think?"

"I want to go for it," said Roddy desperately. "I really do." He looked at their worried faces impatiently. "What's the matter *now*?"

His parents exchanged glances. "Well," said his dad slowly. "There's also the matter of affording it."

"I could get a paper round to help out,"

A Big Decision

Roddy offered. "Or wash cars ... *anything*!"

His mum smiled. "I think the fees for Stadium School might be a bit more than that, Rodrigo," she said. She only used his full name when things were serious.

"Well, in that case, there's no point in me going for the trial, is there?" said Roddy, trying to sound mature. But he couldn't avoid a note of resentment creeping into his voice.

Roddy's dad glanced though all the leaflets he'd been given by Mr Jenkins. "There are some grants and bursaries," he said. "If you got one of those, it would make a big difference."

"How do I do that?" said Roddy.

"Some are awarded on hardship grounds," said his dad. "But they're all linked to ability. Basically, the best students get the most help."

"So I don't just have to get through the trial, I have to get through it *brilliantly*," said Roddy heavily. "Great!"

Hot Prospect

Mrs Jones put her arm round her son. "Dad and I will do a few sums later on tonight," she told him. "We don't want you to miss out any more than you do, but there's only so much money to go round."

"OK," said Roddy quietly.

When he went up to bed that night, his parents stayed at the kitchen table, with lots of bills and papers spread out in front of them. Roddy felt bad that he was putting them through all this worry, but he was worried, too. Surely he wasn't going to lose this opportunity for the sake of money! It seemed so unfair.

The next morning, Roddy came downstairs after both his parents had gone to work. There was a note for him on the table.

Dad and I think you should go for the trial, it said. *We'll try to manage the money.*

It wasn't bad news, but it wasn't entirely

46

A Big Decision

good either. It seemed that if he got in his parents were going to struggle finding the money. But they hadn't said no. That was the most important thing. So he bolted down a bowl of cereal and went straight to the computer. When he googled Stadium School, the website came up straight away.

The school looked just as awesome as he'd remembered from the TV programme. But Roddy didn't want to browse, he was looking for information about the school's trials. When Bryn rang the door bell, Roddy was busy downloading some details. He clattered downstairs and let his friend in.

"Do you want to go swimming later, after we've played football?" asked Bryn. "I brought my gear, just in case."

"Great!" said Roddy. "I'm just on the computer checking out Stadium School. Come with me. I need to print out something."

Hot Prospect

Upstairs, Bryn picked at a scab on his knee. "Let's have a look at the website then," he said.

"Go for it," said Roddy. He got up so Bryn could sit at his desk.

"Hey! They have a cool swimming pool," said Bryn.

"I wonder if I'll get to use it," said Roddy. "Mr Jenkins told Dad I'll have to stay overnight, so I might."

Bryn didn't reply. "What's that you're printing out?" he asked.

"Just some stuff about the trial," said Roddy. "They're sending a letter with all the details, but I want to find out *now* if there's anything I can practise."

Bryn took the page out of the printer and started reading. It said there would be a tour of the school, followed by a big match, where the coaches would be watching carefully. After a

A Big Decision

team-building exercise, they had the evening free to do what they liked. After breakfast the next day, there would be some more football, focusing on skills.

"Well," said Bryn at last. "If you like, I'll help you with your ball skills now."

"Brilliant!" exclaimed Roddy. "Thanks, Bryn." He looked at his friend gratefully and Bryn gave a feeble smile.

"Well, I have to help the future star, don't I?" he said after a pause.

After grabbing a drink, the friends went out into the garden. It was fun practising passing, and they did some headers, too.

"Let's have a go at tackling and dribbling," Roddy suggested.

"Nah," objected Bryn. "I can never get near you."

"Please," said Roddy. "It would really help."

Bryn sighed. "OK. Just for a bit."

Hot Prospect

Roddy couldn't help imagining himself already at Stadium School, training with other stars of the future.

Roddy Jones is working hard in training today, ready for the new season. His dribbling and pace is a big part of his game, and he's running rings around his training partner.

Bryn was right. Roddy *was* better than him at dribbling, and he soon got rather puffed out and very frustrated.

"Want to stop?" asked Roddy.

"No," replied Bryn through gritted teeth. "I've got to win at least *one* ball from you."

Roddy set off, dribbling the ball towards Bryn again. Bryn tried hard to keep his eyes on the ball, but Roddy's quick feet were mesmerising and, as he lunged for the ball, he accidentally caught his friend's leg. Roddy collapsed on the grass and clutched his ankle.

"Sorry," said Bryn awkwardly.

A Big Decision

"You idiot!" shouted Roddy. "The trial is only a couple of weeks away. How am I going to have a chance with an injured ankle?"

"It's not *my* fault," argued Bryn. "You shouldn't have asked me to tackle you."

"I didn't ask you to *foul* me!" yelled Roddy. He got to his feet and winced. "I can hardly put any weight on it now," he groaned. "What if it's a really bad injury? I might never be able to play again."

"Don't be so *dramatic*!" shouted Bryn. "It's not broken or anything, is it?"

"No thanks to you," muttered Roddy, limping painfully towards the house.

Bryn left abruptly, and Roddy didn't bother to say goodbye. He hobbled into the kitchen and sat down at the table.

Liz was there, making lunch. "What's happened to you?" she asked. "Has Bryn gone already?"

Hot Prospect

"Yes," said Roddy, pulling down his sock to reveal a puffy looking ankle. "Look what he did," he added angrily.

"Ah," said Liz unsympathetically, giving his leg a brief glance. "I expect you'll live."

"But it's my trial soon! What if it's not better in time?" The break in Roddy's voice got his sister's attention.

"Oh, yeah!" she said, sounding more concerned. "Well, what's wrong with it? Can you move it?"

Roddy tried swivelling his ankle, and winced.

"Aren't you supposed to put it up, with an ice pack on, or something?" Liz suggested. "Here, prop your leg on this chair."

"We don't have an ice pack," said Roddy, looking dismally at his swelling ankle. "Perhaps I ought to go to casualty."

But Liz was already dunking a tea towel in cold water and wringing it out.

A Big Decision

"Try this," she offered.

Roddy wrapped the cloth round his ankle and then leaned back in the chair. He tried to think positively. Some people must get ill or injured before a trial. Surely they'd let him go on another day?

If only I hadn't made Bryn practise tackles with me, he told himself. *He didn't want to. And he was right. We should have stuck to passing and heading and stuff like that.*

Liz put a glass of squash in front of him. "D'you want me to pass you some pizza?" she offered. She was being so nice to him it was scary. Then the door bell rang. "Hang on. It's probably Izzy. We're going shopping."

Roddy's sister disappeared down the hall and Roddy gingerly felt his ankle through the towel. It really hurt.

"How's the leg?"

It wasn't Izzy. It was Bryn, panting a bit,

looking sheepish, and holding a carrier bag in one hand.

Roddy forced a smile. "It'll be OK," he said, trying to sound more upbeat than he felt.

Bryn dug into the carrier and brought out a bag of frozen peas. "I didn't know if you had anything to put on it," he said. "I've heard that frozen peas are good. You put them on top of a towel or something, so the ice doesn't touch your skin."

"Oh, thanks!" Roddy took the peas. The packet moulded itself neatly around his ankle, and he could feel the cold seeping into his skin.

Bryn stood awkwardly for a moment. "Sorry," he muttered at last.

"It was my fault," Roddy told him straight away. "I was an idiot wanting to practise tackling. It was stupid. I'm just a bit freaked out about the trial and stuff. Sorry."

There was silence for a few moments and

A Big Decision

then Liz came back into the kitchen. "Are you staying for lunch?" she asked Bryn.

Bryn looked at Roddy, who nodded.

"Yeah," Bryn replied, looking happier. "Cheers."

After the peas had melted, and Bryn had gone home, Roddy tried walking up and down on his injured ankle. He had a large bruise, and it was very tender when he touched it. He was glad he and Bryn had made up, but would their friendship survive if his ankle didn't get better in time?

4. Stadium School

Roddy took a look at his bruised ankle. It was the night before the trial and, although the swelling had gone down, it was still painful to the touch. He'd kept off it as much as possible, even though he'd been itching to practise.

"It'll be OK unless I get another knock on it," he told himself, but he wondered how easy it would be to play carefully on such an important day.

It was surprising how much Roddy had to pack for just one night. What with his boots, swimming shorts, wash bag and a change of clothes, he could hardly zip up his rucksack.

He went to bed in good time, as they were going to have a very early start, but no matter how hard he tried, he simply could not get to sleep. He kept looking at the hunched shape of his rucksack and wondering what the next day would bring. Eventually, he managed to drift off, but when his alarm sounded, it felt like he'd only been asleep for a few minutes.

After a quick breakfast, Roddy went out to the car and slung his bag in the boot.

His mum gave him a hug. "Good luck," she said. "Just do your best. No one can ask for more than that."

Roddy was feeling so jittery and nervous he would even have put up with a hug from his sister. It was pretty amazing that she'd got up so early to see him off. But Liz just tapped him on his shoulder. "Good luck, bro," she said. "You can do it!"

Roddy got in and closed the car door. He settled himself into his seat, and fiddled with the knobs on the radio until he found some music that would calm his nerves.

It was a long drive, and by the time they arrived Roddy had given up trying not to be nervous. It had helped to discuss everything he knew about the trial with his dad, and what he should do in every situation they could think of. But as they drew up at the entrance gates, his stomach was churning, and his heart thumped in his chest.

There was a little gatehouse at the entrance, and an official in the trademark green and blue was waiting to see the pass they'd been sent. Roddy's dad handed it over and they waited as the man studied it carefully. After a few moments, he waved them through with a smile.

Stadium School was even more impressive than Roddy had imagined. There were several excellent practice pitches on either side as they made their way up the long drive. They stopped in front of the main building. Large double doors stood open, at the top of a short flight of stone steps. Roddy could see quite a few people milling around, and more were arriving every moment.

"Do you want me to come inside with you?" Roddy's dad asked.

Roddy looked at the other kids. No one else seemed to be going in with a parent.

"It's OK," said Roddy, but his voice was not convincing. He got out of the car and grabbed his rucksack. "I'm fine," he said firmly, slinging the bag over his shoulder, and suddenly he almost was. He gave his dad a brief wave and turned towards the front entrance. He told himself that he didn't need to feel afraid. He'd been *invited* here. He had every right to walk up these steps and enter the building.

Inside, there were several people in blue-and-green sweatshirts, and quite a few people

Hot Prospect

like him, standing around looking lost. Roddy looked about for Peter or Mr Jenkins, but he couldn't see either of them.

"Hi!" said a cheerful young man wearing a Stadium School sweatshirt. "I'm Jason. You're here for the trial, I guess."

Roddy nodded.

"Great!"

Jason crossed Roddy's name off a long list, and picked up the name badge that was ready waiting for him. "I'll take you over to the boys' boarding house. That's where you'll be sleeping tonight," he explained. He led the way along a corridor and out through a side entrance.

Roddy tried to keep his bearings, but after a few twists and turns along the paths he was feeling rather confused. The boarding house was equally impressive. Roddy noticed a large games room downstairs, with pool, table tennis, and table football. Upstairs, there were lots of dormitories, with four beds in each, and a locker for personal belongings.

Roddy pocketed the key from his locker. "I hope I can remember where my room is," he said.

"Don't worry," laughed Jason. "It's confusing to begin with, but you'll soon get your bearings. And if you do get lost, just ask. Anyone in blue and green will soon put you right. Now, come on. We'd better get back for the tour."

"I'd forgotten about that," said Roddy, as they returned to the main building. He really wanted to look round the school, but part of him was impatient to get the trial over with.

"We like to settle people in a bit before we start playing football," explained Jason. "You're bound to feel scared and jumpy when you first arrive. I know *I* did, when I came for

Hot Prospect

my trial. Besides, we want you to enjoy the whole Stadium School experience."

"So, did you used to be a student here?" asked Roddy.

"Still am," said Jason with a grin. "I'm just about to start my final year."

As soon as they got back into the hall, Jason had to go and look after another new arrival. He left Roddy in a small group, all with name badges, and all looking exactly how Roddy felt. No one in the group said anything.

Every now and then, Roddy took a sideways glance at the others. They were his rivals. He didn't know how many places were up for grabs, but there would be loads more kids at the trial than there were places in the school. There were a couple of really tall people, and Roddy wondered if they played in goal. One lad in particular must have been a good foot taller than everyone else.

Stadium School

Roddy tried to guess who the midfielders were, but it was impossible to tell. He drifted over to a notice board at the end of the hall. On it was a list of last term's fixtures, with the results scrawled on in biro.

"Wow!" A pretty girl from his group, with long, blonde hair, had come to look as well. "See who they've been playing! All the best youth teams in the country!"

Roddy turned around. Her name badge said Keira.

"Did you see the programme about the school on TV?" he asked.

Keira grinned. "I recorded it," she said. "Must have watched it about ten times now."

Roddy wished he'd thought of doing that.

"I'll *die* if I don't get in here," she went on. "It's all I've ever wanted. I'm going to be a top international player one day. Well, I hope so anyway," she added with a grin. "That's

Hot Prospect

my dream."

"Mine, too," Roddy said, finding himself smiling back. Her enthusiasm was infectious.

Keira peered at his name badge. "Well, let's hope we *both* get in, Roddy. Then maybe we can both achieve our dream!"

"Yeah," smiled Roddy. If Keira was so positive then Roddy was going to make sure that he was, too.

Just then, the group was called together and Roddy was pleased to see that Jason was going to be taking them on the tour.

"Ask any questions you want," he said. "I'll be showing you all the cool stuff like the pitches and changing rooms, and the boring stuff as well, like the classrooms." He grinned. "By the time you've finished the tour you'll be so determined to come here, you'll breeze through the trial! Come on then." He led the way outdoors and along a gravel path.

Stadium School

Roddy found himself next to a slightly built boy with a mop of thick, black hair. His name badge said Geno. "What position do you play?" Roddy asked, as they made their way along a path.

"I'm a striker," said Geno. "You?"

"Midfield," Roddy told him. "Have you ever been for a trial before?"

"No," said Geno. "But my dad says you just have to concentrate on what you're doing and not worry about anyone else. And playing dirty is absolutely out if you want to get through."

"So, your *dad's* been to a football trial?" said Roddy in surprise. "It wasn't here though, was it? The school hasn't been going that long."

"No," said Geno. "It was in Italy. Years and years ago."

"So, did he get in?" asked Roddy.

Hot Prospect

Geno nodded. "Yes, he did. He's retired from the game now, but I can remember going to watch him when I was little."

"Cool!" said Roddy, wishing his dad had been a professional footballer instead of working for an engineering company. "Who did he play for?"

"Several different clubs in Europe," said Geno. "But he was proudest when he played for Italia."

Roddy stared at him. "Italy? He was an international?"

"Yes." Geno looked embarrassed and proud at the same time.

"What's your surname?" asked Roddy. "I might have heard of him."

"Perotti."

"Of course I've heard of *him*!" Roddy was awestruck. He was walking next to the son of Luca Perotti, one of the greatest Italian players in recent history. He couldn't wait to tell Bryn. Then he felt a pang. If there were many more kids like Geno up for places, Roddy didn't stand a chance. He could just imagine the help and advice Geno must have had all through his life. And of course Stadium School would prefer children of famous parents to a nobody like him.

"Are there many kids here with footballing parents?" he asked.

Geno shrugged. "I don't know. I haven't seen anyone yet. But it doesn't matter," he added, as if he could read Roddy's thoughts. "Just because you have a famous dad doesn't mean you inherit his ability. However much help you have with training, it can't replace talent. Nothing will fool these guys. If you've got what it takes, you'll get in. They don't care who you are, or where you come from. Football is the thing, my dad reckons."

Hot Prospect

Jason took the group past some of the classrooms. "You have to do all the usual lessons, as well as football," he told them. "You take school exams and everything, but you also get wicked football coaching, and loads of match play as well. There are four houses. Charlton, Banks, Moore and Stiles. You get put into a house and throughout your time at school you play matches against the other houses. At the end of each year, the winning house gets the right to sit on the lucky seats at the Stadium pitch."

"Lucky seats?" Roddy said to Geno with a grin. "What are they?"

Several people started laughing, but Jason didn't seem to be joking.

"Come on," he told them. "I'll take you there in a moment."

He led the way out of the school building and into a large block of changing rooms.

"We have separate boys' and girls' changing rooms, of course," said Jason. "And the same for visiting teams, too. We're in the girls' ones at the moment."

The changing rooms were seriously cool. Much better than the scruffy ones at Roddy's old school. Everywhere was tiled, and the polished benches oozed luxury. He'd never thought it would be as good as this!

Jason opened a door to reveal a different room with the same tiled floor. "This connects the two separate changing areas," he explained. "As you know, juniors play mixed matches, so although the doors are usually locked, this room is useful for team talks once you're all changed. Now, have a look at this."

He whisked them through the joining room, and opened another door. Roddy caught his breath in surprise. He'd been expecting the boys' changing room, but this

Hot Prospect

door led outside.

They were facing an avenue of tall, thin trees with branches that almost met overhead, turning the central path into a long, green tunnel. The trees cast a lot of cool shade, and in the light breeze their leaves sounded as if they were advising silence with a long, gentle *ssssh*. Jason led them out into the tunnel. Slowly, everyone fell quiet. About halfway down the avenue, Jason stopped. He turned to face his audience.

"You may already know that Stadium School was built on the site of an old football stadium," he said, his voice sounding oddly flat in the enclosed space. "The school was founded by Jon Masters, who I'm sure you've all heard of. He was one of the first high-earning footballers, and when he retired he wanted to give something back, especially to encourage young players like us."

Stadium School

Jason indicated the young trees either side of them. "This avenue of trees marks the place of the tunnel that the players walked down to reach the pitch," he explained. This ground is where Jon Masters saw his first match as a little boy, and also where he first played professionally. That coincidence made him view this place as really special, and so when he heard that the team had moved to a new stadium, he decided to buy the old one to turn into a school."

"So Jon Masters walked down here," said Roddy, trying to imagine the avenue as a players' tunnel. He could see the two teams lined up, waiting to run on.

"That's right," said Jason. "And if you come down here," he led the way to the end of the avenue, "you can see the pitch."

Roddy gasped. It was the most amazing school pitch he'd ever seen. The grass was

Hot Prospect

perfectly cut, without a blemish on its surface, and at the end of the avenue, off to one side, were a few rows of old, wooden seats. He could see that they must have been part of a large stand at one time, but now they stood alone, looking very odd in the tranquil surroundings. They had all been freshly painted, apart from one of them, which looked as if it had been partly burnt.

"No walking on the pitch," Jason warned, as several people moved forward. "It's only used for matches against outside teams, and for the house finals at the end of the year. If you're not playing, it's out of bounds."

"Which house won last year?" someone wanted to know.

"Moore," said Jason. "My house. But it was very close. These are the lucky seats," he explained. As it's the holidays you can sit here for a few minutes. We like to think that some of the old stadium luck rubs off onto anyone who touches them. Not that one though!" he said hastily, as Roddy made for the nearest seat, the one that hadn't been painted. "Sorry, I should have said. No one sits in that seat, ever. You're allowed to touch it for luck, but not sit in it."

Roddy felt embarrassed. "Why not?" he asked, taking the next one instead.

"Well it's silly, I suppose, but A23 is the seat Jon Masters sat in when he was a child. When he came to restore the seats, he decided to leave that one as it was. There was a fire that swept through the stadium and destroyed most of the stand shortly before he bought it, but he wanted to keep this seat as it was. Somehow it doesn't seem right for us to use it."

"So doesn't *anyone* sit there?" asked a tall boy.

"No," said Jason. "Very occasionally Jon

Hot Prospect

Masters comes to a match. But when he does, he always chooses a different seat. If you come to school here, you'll hear all sorts of ghost stories about the avenue and the seats, but they're not really haunted. Kids just like to make up that sort of thing."

"What sort of ghost stories?" asked a well-built boy, standing some way from Roddy.

Jason looked uncomfortable. "Oh, stuff about the fire, and a phantom footballer," he said. "But you don't want to listen to that sort of rubbish. You're here for a football trial. Come on. I've still got to show you the swimming pool and the gym.

They all got up, and he led them back towards the main school. Roddy trailed his hands over the seats as they left them. If there was any luck to be had from them, he wanted to make sure he got as much of it as possible.

5. At the Trial

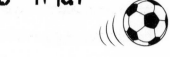

Back at the main building, Roddy's group joined all the other hopefuls in the dining room. While everyone was having a drink, Mr Jenkins appeared. Roddy was very pleased to see a familiar face.

"He was at the summer school day I went on," he explained to Geno excitedly. "He was the one who asked me to come to this trial."

Mr Jenkins clapped his hands to get everyone's attention, and the room fell silent.

"I'm Mr Jenkins, head coach for the juniors," he told them. "Some of you will have met me before. I try to get to as many summer schools as possible, but I don't manage to be

Hot Prospect

at all of them." He paused and looked over the crowd of people in front of him.

"I'd like to welcome you to Stadium School, and to thank you all for coming. I know some of you have travelled long distances to get here. I also know that uppermost in your minds will be the trial, and in a few minutes we'll go over to the changing rooms and get started. But here at Stadium School we can afford to be very choosy, and we like to think that every student who comes here has the right attitude, as well as the right skills to fit in. That is why we invite all our prospective students to stay overnight with us. We can get an idea of what sort of person you are, and hopefully you can find out enough about the school to decide if you'll be happy here."

Mr Jenkins looked to his right, where Jason and a girl from the school were waiting. "OK. Girls, you follow Debbie, and boys, go with

At the Trial

Jason. Your strips are already in the changing rooms. I'll see you out on the field in 20 minutes."

Roddy grabbed his kitbag. His dad had bought him new shin pads with ankle support especially for today. Roddy hoped they'd do the trick and keep his ankle well protected. In the changing room, he took his blue shorts and blue-and-green shirt, and found a space to get changed.

During the guided tour, Roddy had felt quite calm, but as he pulled the shirt over his head, his mouth felt dry. In a few minutes, he would be out there on the practice pitch, doing his best to win a place at this school.

Geno was already changed and, as Roddy finished lacing his boots, his new friend came to stand with him. Geno was looking pale and scared, but there was a determination in his face that Roddy hadn't noticed before.

Hot Prospect

"Well," Roddy said to Geno. "This is it. Good luck."

"Good luck to you, too," said Geno, offering his hand. Roddy hadn't ever shaken hands with a friend before. It felt as if he was crossing some sort of frontier, as if he was growing up in a sudden jerk.

The last boot had been tied, the last shirt put on. Everyone was ready. Roddy and Geno pushed their way out of the changing rooms and onto the pitch. The girls were already there, some standing still and others warming up with stretches or short sprints. They all looked anxious and edgy.

Roddy saw Mr Jenkins approaching and nudged Geno. The players were split up into eight teams of eleven, and Roddy was pleased to have been put with his new friend. The teams had a few minutes to get to know each other and sort out tactics before the matches began. Roddy looked across at their opponents and recognised Keira doing some stretches.

It was a sunny day, but a cool breeze was blowing. The conditions were perfect, and the turf was pretty good, too. Roddy was impressed. For a practice pitch, it was brilliant, better than almost anything he'd played on before. He wouldn't be able to blame the field if he made a mess of things. But Roddy didn't feel as if he would make too many mistakes. Now he was kitted up, he felt really positive and itching to go.

Both teams lined up in a standard 4–4–2 formation. Roddy glanced to the touchline and saw Mr Jenkins watching. He told himself to play like he always did, and not to let the nerves show.

The time has come for Jones to show the world what he can do. The ball comes to him early and he looks up to see where his team-

Hot Prospect

mates are. An opponent is closing in on him fast, but he skips past him with ease and plays a simple ball out to his right, cutting another opponent out with the precision of his pass. Good solid stuff, but nothing spectacular. He's going to have to do more than this to impress the selectors.

Roddy's team lost possession, and he made up a lot of ground to tackle and win back the ball. It was important to show he was hard-working as well as talented, and Roddy was sure he could see Mr Jenkins writing something down in his notebook. Again, under a lot of pressure, he was forced to play a simple pass. Then, just as the ball was knocked back to him, a sliding tackle from an opponent made contact with his injured ankle.

"Ow!" For a few moments Roddy was in agony. He didn't fall, but he stood bent over for a couple of seconds until the pain faded.

At the Trial

He wiped his watering eyes, started to hobble, and then upped his pace to a run. To his relief, the kick didn't seem to have done any lasting damage, but the ball was way up the field now and he had some real work to do to get back into the game.

Roddy wanted an opportunity to run with the ball, to show what he was really capable of. But most people were being a bit selfish. It was natural to want to show what they could do, but one girl on his team was repeatedly holding onto the ball for too long, and then losing it when she should have gone for an easy pass. Roddy wondered whether he should have a word with her about it, but then something else grabbed his attention.

And it's Jones with the pass out to the left wing. Richards is running down the touchline, looking to get the cross in, but a horrendous tackle floors her and the ref blows a furious

Hot Prospect

blast on his whistle. Richards isn't getting up, and appears to be in a lot of pain. Medical staff are rushing onto the pitch. It looks like her part in today's action is over.

Roddy stared with horror at his team-mate on the ground. She'd been tackled by the boy who had kicked Roddy's ankle just a few minutes before. Mr Jenkins was already there, speaking urgently to Jason, the ref. After a few moments, Jason jogged away from the scene of the accident and called everyone over.

"Sarah Richards won't be able to carry on," he said. "So the game will be halted until she's off the pitch. You can all take a break."

"What's wrong?" gasped Keira, trying to catch her breath.

"We won't know until the doctor has arrived," said Jason seriously. "She's had a bad knock. But you guys don't worry about it – you need to keep focused on the trial. Use this time to discuss tactics. One team is a player down, and both teams need to work out how they're going to handle the change."

Everyone was very subdued, and the atmosphere was even worse when an ambulance arrived. Once the girl was loaded in and the ambulance had left, Jason signalled everyone back onto the pitch. Before they started playing again, Mr Jenkins spoke to everyone.

"That was a nasty accident," he said. "But you have to try and put it out of your minds and play on as normal. Footballers get injured all the time. The good news is that I'm sure she's going to be all right. Now, some of you were really impressive before the incident, let's keep it up!"

The boy responsible for the tackle was taken aside and spoken to, but he was allowed to play on. In spite of the girl's injury, Roddy thought it was the right decision. The tackle had looked more misjudged than malicious, and with everyone going all out to impress, accidents were almost bound to happen.

The ref signalled that play should resume. The mood had perceptibly altered and, despite Mr Jenkins's words, everyone was definitely playing with a little less vigour than before.

It could have been me. The words kept echoing round his brain. Roddy told himself to concentrate on the game, but it wasn't easy.

With their numerical disadvantage, Roddy's side began to struggle, and shots started to pour in on their keeper, a Swedish boy called Tom Larsson. But Tom played a blinder in goal and, incredibly, they made it to half-time without conceding. Roddy was sure that the tall goalie would get a place at the school, but his own performance so far had been nothing to shout about.

At the Trial

During half-time, there was very little talking, with everyone's minds still on the horrible accident.

Then Roddy decided to speak up. "We're a player down, but that doesn't mean we can't play well and still win," he said. "They'll be pushing for a goal, so let's aim to get something on the counterattack and make them pay. We can still show the coaches what we can do!"

From the kickoff it was pretty much as Roddy had predicted, with the other team swarming all over their defence, led by Keira, who was running the game for them. She was picking out pass after pass to play to her forwards. Eventually, Roddy's side managed to hold onto the ball for more than a minute, and he found himself with an opportunity to run at the defence.

Jones is off on one of his mazy dribbles,

Hot Prospect

and look, he's going past defenders as if they weren't there, leaving them standing like training dummies! As he reaches the area, he draws back his foot and shoots ... but the ball crashes off the inside of the post and spills out into the box. Perotti is there, and pounces on the free ball, sending it scudding into the goal. Geno Perotti has put his side in front against the odds, but the credit surely has to go to Roddy Jones for that scintillating run!

Roddy glanced at the sidelines to see if Mr Jenkins had taken note of his flash of inspiration, but was shocked to see that he wasn't there! Then he realised that there were three other matches going on, and that there were plenty of other coaches who would be scouting for him. Still, Roddy wished the junior head coach had seen it for himself. There wasn't much time left, and with most of it spent helping out the defence, Roddy didn't

At the Trial

have any more chances to shine.

At the end of the match, Roddy and Geno headed for the changing room together.

"So, what do you reckon?" asked Geno.

Roddy shrugged. "I don't know. It's impossible to tell how much they noticed. I don't think Mr Jenkins was even looking when I made that run."

"It was a good cross you made later on," said Geno. "And they definitely noticed that. I saw one of the assistants making a note."

That cheered Roddy up. At least they'd noticed *something* good that he'd done. "You scored a great goal," he told Geno.

"I *had* to score at least one," said Geno. "I'm a striker. I can't expect to get picked if I can't deliver. You did most of the work for it though."

"But you put it in the net," said Roddy loyally. "That's what counts."

Hot Prospect

"Perhaps," said Geno with a frown. He pulled his shirt over his head and went to take a shower.

Roddy didn't really want to take the Stadium School strip off. While he was wearing it, he could pretend to himself that he'd already got his place at the school. But staff members were waiting to collect the used kit. Reluctantly, Roddy handed it over and went for his shower wondering if he'd *ever* have the chance to play in the blue and green again?

6. School Life

At lunch, Roddy and Geno sat at a table opposite Keira. She was with two girls Roddy hadn't met before, who had been playing in other matches.

"This is great food!" said Keira through a mouthful of chicken pie. "Does anyone know what we're doing next?"

"Swimming?" said Roddy, trying to remember what was on the itinerary.

"Aren't we meeting in the hall?" said Polly, one of the girls with Keira. "Someone said the headmaster was going to talk to us."

"Bor...ing," said the other girl, Tanni.

Keira frowned. "The talk might be interesting," she said.

Hot Prospect

Polly shrugged, and turned to Roddy. "How did you get on in your match?" she asked. "We saw the ambulance from where we were. It was really unsettling. Poor girl, I hope she's OK."

"Mr Jenkins said she would be," Roddy said. "But it was hard to get back into the game afterwards. I think everyone was shaken up."

"What position do you play?" asked Tanni.

Roddy told her and she grinned. "Me, too," she said. "And so do you, don't you, Keira?"

Keira nodded and Tanni smiled again. "There are lots of midfielders here," she said. "Did you score any goals?"

Roddy shook his head. "No, I only got one shot on target and it hit the post."

"Shame," said Tanni, looking pleased rather than sympathetic. "I got one in and had several shots at goal. Quality always shows," she bragged.

School Life

"Well, if we hadn't been down to ten players..." said Roddy. But he left the comment hanging. There was no point in arguing over who had been best. It was Mr Jenkins who would decide.

"Come on, let's find a good seat in the hall," said Keira, getting to her feet.

"OK," agreed Roddy. "Come on, Geno, leave that!"

Geno had been concentrating on eating. He scowled at Roddy, scraped up the last bit of potato, then put his knife and fork tidily at the edge of his plate, making Roddy wait. "OK," he said at last, with an infuriating grin, glancing at Roddy's messy, abandoned plate.

Roddy grinned back. Geno might be slightly built, but he obviously wasn't the type to be pushed around.

There was still plenty of room in the hall, so they got good seats near the front. After a

Hot Prospect

few minutes, Mr Jenkins came in, accompanied by a man dressed in a dark suit.

"Hello, everyone," said the man in the suit. "My name is Paul Wender, and I'm the head of Stadium School."

Roddy was surprised. He had assumed that the head would be wearing blue and green like everyone else, but he was dressed like a bank manager.

"I hope you all enjoyed the trial this morning," the head went on. "Mr Jenkins tells me that the standard this year is very high, which is terrific. We like to keep ahead in the league we play in, but as more and more top clubs improve their youth squads, the opposition is getting tougher."

"We accept about 50 students each year," Mr Wender told them. "And as there are almost 100 people here today, unfortunately many of you won't get places. I'm sorry we can't take more. However," he went on, "those of you who miss out mustn't think of yourselves as failures. Just to have been offered a trial here means you have heaps of talent. If you're serious about making it as a professional footballer then you still have a chance that a club will sign you at some point. And if you think you've performed badly this morning, don't give up hope quite yet," he said.

Roddy crossed his fingers, and Geno did the same.

"You might not think we've seen your potential," said Mr Wender. "But we notice a lot more than you may realise. And remember," he continued, "we're looking for character as well as skill. You might be the best striker in the world, but if you're not a team player we'll think very hard before taking you on."

Hot Prospect

Roddy thought about the girl in his match who had refused to pass to him several times. He was sure she'd only held onto the ball to try and impress Mr Jenkins, but she'd been tackled and, as a result, they'd almost given away a goal. How on earth would the staff decide if her style of play was influenced by being on trial, or if she was usually selfish with passing?

"Tomorrow morning you'll be doing some activities that will give you a chance to demonstrate more of your skills, and Mr Jenkins will show you our media centre. But for the rest of today," said the head, "relax and enjoy yourselves. We want your visit here to be fun as well as challenging. And now I'll leave you in the capable hands of Mr Jenkins and his team."

The head left and Mr Jenkins smiled. "Right then," he said. "We have some exciting activities for you this afternoon, but first I thought you'd like to know that Sarah Richards, who was injured this morning, is OK. The hospital tells me that she has a simple fracture, which has been put in plaster. She won't be able to play for quite a while, but we've promised her another trial when she's fit."

"That's good," Roddy said quietly to Geno.

"She might not want to come back," said Geno. "A broken leg is a horrible injury to get. It's enough to put anyone off."

Roddy was surprised. He couldn't imagine *anything* changing his mind about playing, but then he'd never broken his leg.

"To help you get to know the school a bit better, we thought we'd organise a short orienteering session this afternoon," Mr Jenkins continued. "I hope you'll find it fun, but you will be timed, so you'll have to be fast

Hot Prospect

if you want to win the prize. It'll be a good test of your fitness, and teamwork as well. Then there will be a chance to have a swim, and after tea you'll have free time in the boarding houses. Our students have lots of fun here after school hours. There's table football, pool and computer games, including plenty of football ones of course, so there's never any reason to be bored."

"What about TV?" asked a boy near the front.

"Each boarding house *does* have a TV set in the common room," said Mr Jenkins. "But to be honest they don't get watched an awful lot ... except for when there are football matches!"

Several people laughed.

"For the orienteering, you'll need to get into groups of four," said Mr Jenkins. "So let's see how quickly you can organise yourselves."

School Life

Keira wanted to stay with the two girls she'd met, so Roddy and Geno hooked up with Ali, a goalie, and John, who'd been on the wing in their team earlier. Each group was given a compass and a map of the school and its grounds. They had to get their cards stamped by a member of staff at each checkpoint they navigated to, and there were clues to collect as well. Everyone was told to meet back in the hall afterwards.

"Each clue is a letter," said Mr Jenkins. "Once you have them all, see if you can make them into a word or phrase. And if you haven't finished by three o'clock, then just come back here anyway, otherwise it'll be too late to fit in a swim. Good luck, everyone!"

Roddy hadn't done any orienteering before, but Ali had, and he showed them how to use the compass to follow their instructions. They raced off to the first checkpoint, leaving

Hot Prospect

several of the other teams standing. But after collecting a couple of letters, they seemed to be lost.

"Let's go round by the pool," said Ali. "We might find the way to the next checkpoint there."

"No!" said Roddy impatiently, seeing their early lead slipping away. "Look at the map! We need to return to the main house. The checkpoint is round the back."

Ali didn't want to do that, but he was outvoted.

"I think you're better at leading than Ali," panted Geno as they sprinted along the path. "He hasn't been paying attention to the map."

They were soon back on track, and heading for the checkpoint manned by Justin.

"There's one group ahead of you," he told them as they raced up. He stamped their card. "But not by much. You might overtake them if you hurry."

They all needed to catch their breath, but Roddy urged them on. "Hurry up!" he said. "We've almost done it!"

By the time they picked up the last clue and got back to the hall they were exhausted, and to their dismay they found that the other team had already cracked the code.

"There were two words, not one," Mr Jenkins explained. "But never mind. You were the second-fastest team to finish. Well done!"

Geno looked at the letters again. "Of course," he said after a few moments. "The letters make *blue* and *green*!"

The winning team members got a football each. Roddy eyed them enviously. He would have loved a new football.

After the orienteering almost everyone wanted to swim, so the pool was packed. It was an opportunity to relax, and for the first

Hot Prospect

time that day Roddy felt as if he didn't have anything to prove. Afterwards, the mood stayed with them. People chatted more openly with each other, as if they weren't rivals any more.

Roddy was starting to feel very at home at Stadium School, and it looked as if he wasn't the only one. A group of boys loitering by the serving hatch started singing football songs and another group took an orange from the servery, and started an impromptu game of football.

"That boy, Jack, by the door, is a brilliant midfielder," said someone behind Roddy. "He's sure to get a place. There's no one to beat him. And his dad knows the headmaster."

"He may be good, but he's a thug," said another. "I had enough trouble with bullies at my last school. I don't want to be bullied if I come here."

School Life

Roddy looked towards the door and saw a solidly built, brown-haired boy. He turned to Geno. "I wish my dad knew the head. Or owned a football club, or had been a professional footballer like yours."

"But I bet there'll be no pressure from your parents if you don't get in," Geno said. "I expect your parents will be proud of you whatever happens."

Something in his voice made Roddy look at him again. "Will your dad be angry then, if you don't pass the trial?" he asked.

"He won't be *angry*," Geno told Roddy. "But I know how disappointed he'll be, and that's almost worse. I'll feel dreadful if I let him down. Since I got this trial, he's been going on about how I'll play for Italy like he did. But I'm nowhere near as good as he was."

Roddy hadn't thought it would be possible to feel sorry for Geno, but now he did. "Come

Hot Prospect

on," he said cheerfully. "The trial's over now. We can't change anything."

"OK," agreed Geno. "You're right. Let's have our tea. Then I'll challenge you to a game of table football, if you like."

"You're on!" said Roddy. "Food first, then football!"

7. Evening

After Roddy and Geno had eaten until they were totally stuffed, they left the dining room and made their way back to the boarding house. To their disappointment, they found that they weren't sharing a room. Geno would be sleeping at the far end of Roddy's corridor. But it wasn't time for bed yet.

Downstairs, there was a queue of boys waiting to play table football. Mr Clutterbuck the housemaster intervened to avoid any argument. "First to three goals wins," he said. "Winner stays on. While you're waiting, why not play table tennis, or go on the computers?"

The action was fast and furious, with the

Hot Prospect

ball rattling into the goal time and time again. It wasn't long before it got to Roddy's turn. He was up against a blond boy that he'd noticed earlier in the day.

"Come on, Simon!" yelled someone nearby.

Simon glanced at Roddy and grinned. "Prepare to eat dirt," he said. "Ready?"

"Ready."

Neither of them was going to give away an easy goal. Roddy had played a few times before, and it looked like his opponent had, too. For a few minutes they battled away, before Simon sent the ball crashing into Roddy's goal.

"Hard luck," said Geno. But there was no time to reply. As soon as the ball was back in play, Simon was on the offensive, and Roddy had to work hard to keep the ball out of his half. He tried distracting Simon with a few dummies, then passed quickly and fired it into the goal. Geno cheered, and Simon shook his head.

"All right, I'll start playing properly now," he said.

They were both giving it everything they'd got, and everyone else was getting a bit fed up of waiting when Simon scored a lucky goal, shooting the whole length of the pitch with his goalie. The third goal soon followed, but Simon offered Roddy his hand as a gesture of respect for a worthy opponent.

Roddy left the table reluctantly and rejoined Geno.

"You were really good!" said Geno.

Roddy smiled. "Thanks. Shall we have a go at table tennis now?" he said.

Geno was much better than Roddy at that. "Fair enough," said Roddy after Geno had thrashed him twice. "But I bet I can beat you on the computer."

Hot Prospect

It was late when Mr Clutterbuck came to tell everyone it was bedtime. No one wanted to go, but as they made their way back to the dormitories, Roddy realised how tired he was. It had been a very full day, and it felt as if he'd arrived weeks ago, not just this morning.

"Whatever happens, it's been great," said Geno.

"I wouldn't have missed it for anything," agreed Roddy.

"Come on now," said Mr Clutterbuck. "Into bed before you fall asleep in the corridor. I don't want to come along in the morning and find you in a pile on the floor."

"Mr Clutterbuck's OK, isn't he?" said Roddy.

"I wouldn't mind him for a housemaster," agreed Geno.

At the top of the stairs, Roddy and Geno saw Simon.

"We're going to have a pillow fight later.

Do you want to join us?" he asked. "We're in room three."

"Sure," agreed Roddy. He'd never had a pillow fight before and it sounded fun.

"What about you?" Simon turned to Geno. "Are you up for it?"

"No, thanks," said Geno quickly.

"Afterwards we're going to have a midnight feast," said Simon. "I have a few chocolate bars, and some people smuggled up food from the dining hall. It'll be a laugh, but we'll need to take turns to keep a watch for Clutterbuck."

"Sounds good," said Roddy. "See you later."

Geno watched Simon disappear into his room and turned to Roddy. "Don't get into trouble," he warned. "You don't want to do anything to risk your place here."

Roddy hadn't thought of that. He considered it for a moment and then patted

Hot Prospect

Geno on the shoulder. "You worry too much. This is a boarding school. Aren't pillow fights and midnight feasts what it's all about? They're not going to miss out on the best footballers for the sake of a midnight feast! Are you sure you don't want to come?"

"Well..." Geno was obviously torn.

"I'll swing by your room before I join Simon, shall I?" offered Roddy. "Then if you change your mind, we can go together."

"OK," agreed Geno at last. "It does sound fun. I'll see you later."

Roddy was just about to get into bed when his phone beeped and he got a text. *Hope U had a gd day*, it said. It was from Bryn.

Roddy texted back. *Yeah tks. This place is awesome! C U 2mrw*. He was looking forward to telling Bryn all about it.

Then he received another text from his parents. Mr Clutterbuck was at the door by the time he'd replied. "Straight to sleep now," he said. "Don't forget, there's a lot happening tomorrow before you go home. We're all going to be up bright and early." Then he switched off the light and closed the door.

The boys lay quietly, getting used to the darkness in the room. Slowly, Roddy began to see the outlines of the furniture. A bit of light was coming under the door so it wasn't totally black. It was very different from his room at home, where the streetlight shone through his curtains and traffic noises carried on all night long.

Here, in the middle of Stadium School's parkland, they were some way from the road. Roddy thought he'd never be able to sleep in such silence. The only sound was the wind in the nearby trees. Hearing it reminded him of the tree tunnel and the preserved stadium seats they'd been shown earlier in the day. The whole thing had been rather creepy, especially the charred seat that no one ever sat in. He found himself wondering if something awful had happened there that they hadn't been told about.

Roddy lay quietly for a little while longer, wondering when the pillow fight was supposed to start. He'd forgotten to ask Simon, and he didn't know if any of the other boys in his room had been invited. Perhaps he'd get up in a few minutes and go along to room three to find out. If Mr Clutterbuck was still around, he could always say he was going to the bathroom, and had forgotten the way.

He stretched out in the comfortable bed and relaxed under the duvet. He told himself he'd wait another five minutes. He could look at the time on his phone, but it was on his bedside locker, and he couldn't be bothered to reach out and get it. In fact he was getting so comfortable, he'd have to do something to make sure he didn't nod off. But, as Roddy was trying to think of a way to keeping awake, he slipped further away from consciousness. And soon he fell into a deep, dreamless sleep.

8. Home Again

The boys woke up to strong sunshine pouring into the room. Mr Clutterbuck was opening the curtains. Roddy groaned.

"Time to get up," said Mr Clutterbuck. "Don't go back to sleep now, will you?" Then he turned and left the room.

Suddenly, Roddy remembered the pillow fight and midnight feast. He'd missed them! He felt really annoyed with himself for falling asleep so quickly. He'd cheated himself out of some good boarding-school fun, and Simon would think he'd wimped out.

It was tempting to drift back to sleep, but Roddy knew he had to get up, so he threw off his duvet and sat up. The other three boys

Home Again

looked bleary eyed, too. Roddy tumbled out of bed, and made his way to the bathroom. Simon was there, coming out of the shower.

"Sorry about missing last night," said Roddy, feeling rather sheepish. "It was stupid, but I fell asleep. Was it fun?"

Simon laughed. "Nothing happened," he said. "I think we *all* fell asleep. At any rate, I wasn't aware of any pillow fight going on..."

"You're joking!" said Roddy feeling much less stupid now.

After his shower, Roddy saw Geno in the corridor.

"So much for your plans," Geno laughed. "I got tired of waiting, so I came along to your room to see what the hold up was."

"Did you?" said Roddy, amazed. "I didn't hear a thing."

"You were all snoring away," said Geno. "So I went back to bed."

Hot Prospect

"Well, we didn't miss anything,' Roddy told him. "Apparently Simon's room fell asleep, as well."

⚽ ⚽ ⚽

Before they went for breakfast, Mr Clutterbuck gathered everyone together. "I'm glad you had a good time in the boarding house last night," he said. "But your parents are coming to collect you around midday, so there won't be time for any more table football."

"What a shame," said Roddy, "I really enjoyed it."

"Don't forget to strip your beds and leave the bedding on the corridor floor." A collective groan went up and he smiled. "This isn't a hotel. If you're lucky enough to get a place here, you'll soon become used to changing your own sheets."

By the time they'd done their jobs and packed, Roddy was getting hungry. He hoisted

Home Again

his rucksack onto his shoulder, and in no time he was downstairs. After a couple of minutes, Geno arrived, and they went over to the main building together. As soon as they'd dumped their bags in the entrance, they went into the dining hall.

Roddy was surprised that there was a full fry-up on offer. He'd imagined it would just be healthy cereal and fruit, but they were going to need a lot of energy if they were playing football every day.

After breakfast, there were some ball-control exercises, which Roddy did really well at. He and Keira were two of the best at dribbling, although she had the edge when it came to scooping up loose balls.

Then Mr Jenkins had a treat for them. "I'm going to show you how helpful technology can be in improving your game," he said, leading them to a building they hadn't visited

Hot Prospect

before. In the media centre, full-time students had the opportunity to watch video footage of their own games and pick up on areas in need of improvement.

"As well as watching the game, like you would on TV at home, we can turn each piece of action into a computer simulation," explained Mr Jenkins. "This allows us to view it from any angle, or to follow a specific player. It can be very helpful, and you can break down each person's playing statistics as well, to see how effectively they use the ball."

"Wow," said Ali.

Everyone was very impressed with the cutting-edge technology being used, and longed to see themselves on the screen. Though of course that wasn't going to happen unless they got a place at the school. Instead, they watched some footage of the Stadium School first team from the year before, playing

Home Again

against Manchester United under-18s. Mr Jenkins showed them edited highlights to demonstrate how the system worked, and drew virtual circles and arrows to help his explanation. Roddy and Geno agreed that it was one of the coolest bits of technology they'd ever seen.

All too soon, it was time to think about heading home. Roddy and Geno wandered back to the main building together. Roddy felt a bit subdued. It wasn't only that this had been two of the best days of his life, and he was sad to leave the school. It was also hard to leave the new friends he'd made, especially Geno. Would he ever see him again, or Simon, or Keira?

Roddy went over to the pile of bags and picked up his rucksack.

"There are loads of cars here already," said Geno, looking out of the open door.

Hot Prospect

He was right, and more were arriving every minute. Roddy felt his mood lift. He couldn't wait to see his dad. He had so much to tell him.

"Roddy?"

"What?"

It was Geno, with his phone in his hand. "Can I have your number?" he asked. "Maybe we could meet up some time."

"OK!" Roddy felt very pleased. He hadn't wanted to ask, in case Geno had thought Roddy only wanted to hook up with him because of his famous dad.

"I know you live in Wales and I live in London, but you never know," said Geno, keying in Roddy's number. "You might come to London some time."

"And you might come to Wales," said Roddy grinning, but that didn't seem likely.

"There's my car!" Geno picked up his bag and started for the door. Then he stopped and looked back at Roddy. "Good luck," he said seriously. "I hope you get in. You deserve to – you're really good."

"Thanks," said Roddy. "You, too. Let me know how you get on, OK?"

"OK."

"Bye then."

"Bye."

Geno went down the steps and onto the gravel drive. Roddy stood in the doorway and watched. He looked at the smart, black Mercedes Geno was heading for. Roddy had hoped to catch a glimpse of Geno's famous father, but there was just a woman in the car. She leaned over and opened the passenger door. Geno went round to the boot and put his bag in before climbing into the front seat. He looked back at the school and waved. Roddy waved back. Then the car pulled away, and in a few moments it had gone.

Hot Prospect

Roddy took his rucksack and sat on the steps to wait for his dad. After a few minutes, the car arrived.

"Hey! Roddy!"

He turned round. It was Keira.

"Are you off?"

"Yeah. My dad's here."

"Oh, right. Well, goodbye then. See you some time."

"Yes." Roddy wasn't going to say it. After all, she was a rival midfielder, but then he couldn't help himself. "Good luck," he said.

Keira's face lit up and she grinned. "Good luck to you, too," she said. "Really, I mean it."

"And me," agreed Roddy. "But I must go now. Bye!"

Roddy crossed the drive. His dad was already out of the car. He looked as if he wanted to hug his son, but although part of him wanted to do the same, Roddy held back.

Home Again

"Well," said Roddy's dad. "How was it?"

Roddy didn't reply until they were both in the car. He sank back in his seat and sighed. Now it had come to it, he wasn't sure how to explain. He had so many mixed-up feelings about the past two days.

"I just..." he said, searching for the right words. "I just want to go there *so* badly." For an instant, he was afraid he might burst into tears, but that would be pathetic, so he swallowed several times and bit his lip. "It was... great," he added and closed his eyes.

And it *had* been great, every minute of it, a sort of paradise for football-mad people like him. He'd been so lucky to get the trial, and he was incredibly grateful for the experience. But he knew that after this glimpse of football heaven, his ordinary, humdrum existence would never be the same again.

9. The Waiting Game

Back at home again, life felt unreal. Roddy couldn't settle down to anything. Even playing football had lost some of its appeal. Every time he looked at a ball, Roddy started wondering when he would hear if he'd got a place at Stadium School. He did his best to wait patiently, but it was *agony* not knowing. And everyone's lives seemed to be moving on, while his was stalled. His sister, Liz, had passed her GCSEs and was going to the local sixth-form college. And Bryn had already been shopping with his mum to buy his new Valley Comp uniform.

"I got some new football boots today," he told Roddy one afternoon. "And I need to

The Waiting Game

break them in. Shall we have a kick about in the park?"

"OK," agreed Roddy. "I'll go and get mine." He was still using the ones he'd worn to the trial. "Dad said it isn't worth getting new ones until I know where I'm going."

"Still not heard then?" asked Bryn sympathetically.

Roddy shook his head. "They said it would be about ten days, and that was up yesterday."

"I'm sure you'll find out soon," said Bryn.

"Probably," agreed Roddy. But he knew that the more time went by, the less likely he was to get a place. Surely they'd write to all the people they had accepted first? Roddy wondered if he should text Geno to find out if he'd heard anything. But what if he'd already received a letter, and got in? Roddy knew he'd feel terrible. No, it would be best not to text. Not yet, anyway. He ought to forget about

Hot Prospect

Geno and concentrate on his friends at home, not on someone he'd probably never meet again.

Bryn was the best mate he could have, but Roddy knew that part of him was hoping he wouldn't get a place. Then they could go to Valley Comp together as they'd always planned. They'd keep their brilliant footballing partnership. They'd get into the first team and be heroes right up the school. And, at 17, they'd both turn pro with a local side and work their way up until, at last, they'd go out onto the pitch at Wembley, playing in the final of the World Cup.

It was a good dream, a *great* dream, and Roddy didn't blame Bryn for hanging onto it. But Roddy had been tantalised by a different dream, one where Bryn didn't figure, and that was difficult for both of them.

They went over to the park and had a kick

about. Roddy took an interest in Bryn's new boots, and asked all the right questions. They discussed studs, and what the Valley Comp pitch would be like, and hoped the changing rooms would be better than the ones at their old primary school.

Then Bryn asked about the pitch at Stadium School and Roddy came alive with enthusiasm. "It's better than loads of championship pitches," he told him. "It's got under-soil heating so the grass doesn't get frosty in the winter, and the drainage is brilliant, too. Jason told me that it hardly gets muddy at all!"

"I wish I'd been there," sighed Bryn.

"I know," agreed Roddy. "And I wish you'd been there when Jason was telling us about the stadium seats. I almost sat in the charred one. He looked *horrified*, as if I was going to get *killed* or something. It's obviously really important for some reason."

Hot Prospect

"Valley Comp has a ghost," offered Bryn.

"Really?" said Roddy. "Liz never said anything about it."

"You know David, the kid who lives in my road," said Bryn. "His brother goes there, and he told him there's a ghost in the boys' bogs."

"Seriously?" said Roddy.

"Dunno," said Bryn. "It's probably not true anyway."

There was silence for a few moments while each was deep in his own thoughts.

"Bet I can hit that tree from here with the ball," said Roddy, changing the subject. He was fed up with talking about schools. After all, it *was* the summer holidays. They should forget about school, any school, until the autumn.

"Hey, Roddy!" It was Ian, a boy from round the corner. "A bunch of us are going over to the recreation ground for a game of football. Do you want to come? You can be on my team if you like," he added hopefully.

Roddy looked at Bryn. "You up for it?" he asked.

"Why not?"

"OK," said Roddy. "As long as Bryn's on my side."

The recreation ground was a short way from Roddy's home. The grass was clumpy and badly looked after. Kids rode their bikes there, churning great grooves when it was wet and sometimes people walked their dogs over it, even though they weren't supposed to. It paid to look out for dog mess before you started playing, but Roddy and Bryn could never be bothered.

Jones is coasting today, oozing class as always but not giving it his all. After his recent trial with a big team he's lost his passion for the game at this level and, to be fair, it's not teaching him anything any more. It can only be

Hot Prospect

a matter of time before a big club picks up the young star. It'll be a sad day for his current team-mates, but Jones is surely destined for bigger things.

"See you tomorrow?" said Bryn as they pulled off their boots.

"Yeah," said Roddy with a sigh. He would never admit it to Bryn, but his Stadium School experience had shown him that football could be much more exciting with players of his own standard. "Liz wants to go shopping. We'll have the house to ourselves so bring some computer games over."

"Great!"

"See you about ten thirty?"

Bryn nodded. "I'll be there."

They lived at opposite sides of the recreation ground, so while Bryn headed off to the gate in the far side, Roddy went along the path and out into the street.

The Waiting Game

He walked up the road and round the corner, where the parade of shops was. He hesitated by the newsagents and wondered whether to go in and buy a Lucky Bag. They were pretty naff by and large, and he'd grown out of them really, but he couldn't help indulging in them occasionally. There was always the hope that you'd find something good inside. Once he'd got a mini Frisbee that had flown for miles.

Roddy settled on a promising bag, checked it said BOY on it, paid and went back outside. He was tempted to open it straight away but decided it would keep until later.

At home, he chucked his boot bag under the coat pegs and went upstairs. Then the front door slammed.

"Liz! Liz, are you up there?"

His sister threw open her bedroom door. "What is it?" she yelled.

Hot Prospect

"I want to speak with you," said Mum. "Can you come here, please?"

Roddy listened as his sister stomped down the stairs and into the hall. He was just about to open the Lucky Bag when Mum called up again.

He stood at the top of the landing, looking down at his mother and sister. "What do you want?" he asked.

Mum was waving an envelope. "Look!" she said. "There's a letter for you."

Roddy started slowly down the stairs, his heart pounding in his chest. "How can there be a letter?" he asked. "There wasn't one this morning."

"It was put through next-door's letter box," said Liz. "And they brought it round. I've already explained to Mum. It's not my fault."

"I didn't say it was," said their mum patiently. "I just wondered about it, that's all."

The Waiting Game

"So can I go back upstairs now?" asked Liz.

"Don't you want to find out what Roddy's letter says?" said Mum.

Liz rolled her eyes, but Roddy wasn't taking any notice of her. His legs had suddenly got a life of their own. He fizzed downstairs and took the letter. The large envelope was made of high-quality paper, and the unmistakable blue-and-green logo was in the top left-hand corner. This was the moment he'd been waiting for, but now it had arrived he didn't dare open the envelope. His future was inside.

"You open it," he said, offering it to his sister.

"No way!" said Liz. "You have to do it."

"OK." Roddy steeled himself to rip open the envelope. He took out the sheet of paper and looked at it. The words blurred on the page and he couldn't make out what they said. He took a deep breath and concentrated.

Hot Prospect

Dear Mr Jones,

We are delighted to inform you that you have been allocated a place at Stadium School, starting on September 2nd.

If you would like to accept, please let us know by August 25th. If we do not hear from you, your place will be offered to someone else.

Roddy read the letter, and then he read it again. When he finally spoke, his voice came out in a squeak. "I've got in," he said.

"What?"

"Oh, Roddy!"

"I've done it!" he said, his voice now loud and triumphant, with a broad grin stretching his face. "I've only gone and got in!"

10. A New School

Roddy couldn't stay in the hall. He felt short of air and needed to get outside. He thrust the letter into his mum's hand, ignored her protests, and made for the back door. On the way out, he grabbed his old, worn football. The next moment he was in the little back garden, with its small patio and patch of scruffy grass. He took several deep breaths and looked about him, as if he'd never really noticed his surroundings before.

He'd played football out here since he'd been tiny. There were photographs in an album of him in the back garden as a toddler, with a football at his feet. There was even one of him and Liz playing together, something

Hot Prospect

she'd never do now. And there were loads of pictures of him and his dad, and some with his mum. He remembered the goal they'd bought him one birthday. It fell over if you scored, but he'd loved it, and had imagined himself as an international player even then.

Roddy looked down at the ball in his hands. It was getting very scruffy – he needed a new one really. He shouldn't dribble it down the street so much. Tarmac wasn't good for footballs.

He started working the ball, bouncing it on the patio, kneeing it higher, and up onto his head. He had it under control, like his feelings. It was as if he couldn't quite allow himself to feel the joy of having got a place, in case it wasn't true. But it *was* true! He *had* got in. He'd read the letter himself!

Roddy's feelings suddenly bubbled up, and overflowed. As the ball bounced higher, he gave it an *almighty* kick, and let out a wordless bellow of excitement.

For a moment, he thought the ball was going to hit the shed window, but it skimmed over the roof, over the fence and out of the garden into the road. Roddy heard the hollow bounce as it hit the roof of a parked car. He heard it bounce again, this time onto the road, and then start to roll down the hill.

"Let it go," he said into the empty garden. "Let some other kid have it. I don't need it any more."

He turned to go back indoors and saw his mum and sister staring at him. In a rush, he remembered about the money. Had the letter said anything about a bursary? He couldn't remember, and he couldn't read his mum's expression at all.

"Mum!" he said in agony. "Can we afford it?" He held his breath. He couldn't bear to be cheated out of his place at the last moment. He'd tried so hard. How could he not go now?

His mum was shaking her head, and Roddy felt his heart stop. "How can we say no, Rodrigo?" she said softly. "We'll manage somehow."

"Are you sure?" he asked.

She was smiling at him, and he could see that she meant it. He went over and gave her a hug. "Thanks," he said, so full of emotion he was almost in tears. It was going to be all right.

That night there was loads to think about. Along with the letter was a big list of things Roddy would need at his new school. He pored over it with his parents. As well as school clothes and shoes, he would need everyday clothes for after hours. He could take his own duvet cover to make his room more homely if he wanted, a few books, an MP3 player and no more than two computer games. All the sports

A New School

kit he needed would be available from the school shop, which had second-hand clothing as well as new.

"We'll go shopping in the morning," Roddy's mum said.

"OK," agreed Roddy. Shopping for school clothes wasn't usually his favourite activity, but this time he couldn't wait.

Roddy was going to tell Bryn his news straight away, but what with all the excitement, he didn't have time. His father suggested going out for a celebration supper, and it was late when they got back.

Roddy said goodnight and went up to his room. He still couldn't believe it. He wasn't going to start at Valley Comp in a few weeks' time. He didn't need to care about what a huge school it was, and if he was good enough for the football team. He was *too* good for it. That was the truth. He was so good that

Hot Prospect

Stadium School wanted him to go there instead!

He pulled out his phone, and looked at the time. Bryn might not be asleep yet. He really ought to call and let him know – it would be mean not to. And then he caught his breath. Of course! He'd invited Bryn round in the morning to play computer games. They wouldn't be able to do that now because he was going shopping instead. Now he really *had* to phone him.

After a few moments Bryn answered Roddy's call.

"What?" he said in a sleepy voice.

"Sorry," said Roddy. "Were you asleep?"

"Sort of," said Bryn. "It doesn't matter. What do you want?"

"It's just that we can't go on the computer tomorrow," Roddy told him awkwardly. "I have to go shopping instead."

A New School

"Oh, never mind," said Bryn. "We can do it some other time."

"True," admitted Roddy slowly. "It's just that I've got to get my school stuff, and tomorrow's the best day."

"Oh, right."

There was a pause.

"So you got a letter then?" Bryn asked at last.

"Yes," said Roddy. "It was waiting for me when I got home from the recreation ground."

There was another pause and then Bryn's voice came accusingly down the phone.

"You could have phoned me before," he said crossly. "I've been really worried about going to Valley Comp on my own. If it'd been me, I'd have told you straight away. Sorry you didn't get in though," he added after a moment.

"No, it's not that," said Roddy quickly.

Hot Prospect

"I *did* get in. That's just it. I'm going to Stadium School on September 2nd!"

There was a long silence down the phone.

"Are you still there?" Roddy asked anxiously.

"Yes," said Bryn. His voice sounded very flat. Then it lifted, as if he was making a big effort. "Well, congratulations," he said. "You must be really pleased."

"I am," said Roddy, feeling terrible for his friend. "Look, come round tomorrow afternoon will you? We can play on the computer then. OK?"

"Maybe," said Bryn. "Well, OK. I will. Look, I do mean it. Congratulations and all that. It's just a bit of a shock," he explained. "Don't get me wrong, but I thought you hadn't done it."

"Me, too," agreed Roddy, grateful that Bryn was coming round. "I was *sure* I hadn't."

A New School

"You'll have to give me your autograph," said Bryn. "Before you go."

"Don't be soft," said Roddy, trying not to laugh. "Who'd want my autograph?"

"When you're famous," said Bryn. "I want to be able to say that I knew you first, that I got the first autograph of the great Roddy Jones."

"Idiot," said Roddy.

"Loser," said Bryn.

"Night then."

"Night."

Roddy snapped his phone shut and smiled to himself. Everything was OK. Bryn was still his mate, even if they weren't going to the same school.

Roddy was just about to get into bed when he noticed something on his desk. He went over and picked it up. It was the Lucky Bag he'd bought that afternoon. It seemed a

Hot Prospect

lifetime ago. He looked at it and tossed it back onto his desk. He didn't need a Lucky Bag any more.

⚽ ⚽ ⚽

September 2nd finally arrived. It was a Sunday, so the whole family was able to go to Stadium School with Roddy. Even Liz decided she didn't want to miss out.

The car was full of bags and boxes, and they were just about to set off when Bryn came running up the road.

"Wait, Dad!" yelled Roddy. He jumped out of the car and ran to meet his friend.

"I was afraid I was going to miss you," said Bryn. "I wanted to give you this." He held out a carrier bag and Roddy took it.

"Thanks," he said. "What is it?"

"Just an ankle support." Bryn sounded embarrassed. "I thought it might be useful, you know ... no hard feelings or anything."

A New School

Roddy didn't know what to say. They never gave each other presents. They didn't even bother with birthday cards any more. But somehow Bryn had managed to make this moment special. He was simply the best mate ever. "Thanks!" Roddy said again, wishing he'd thought to get something for Bryn. He could have hugged him, but that was impossible, so he punched him on his arm instead. Then they grinned at each other.

"Good luck at your new school and everything," said Bryn.

"You, too," echoed Roddy.

They both made a fist and knocked them together.

"See you at half term," said Roddy.

"Yeah."

Roddy sprinted back to the car. As they drove off, he wound down his window and leaned out. "Get in the team!" he yelled.

Hot Prospect

A broad grin stretched Bryn's face. "You, too!" he shouted.

In another moment they had gone round the corner, and Bryn was out of sight. Roddy settled back into his seat, hugging the carrier bag to his chest. It was still difficult to believe, but it was true. He was on his way to the biggest adventure of his life. Roddy Jones was going to Stadium School!